UNITARIAN CHURCH OF EDMONTON
12530 - 110 AVENUE
EDMONTON, AB.   T5M 2L5

CANCELLATION

Half for You

Story by Meyer Azaad

Pictures by Naheed Hakeeget

CAROLRHODA BOOKS INC.

MINNEAPOLIS, MINNESOTA U.S.A.

In the spring of the year the world is reborn.
Seeds sprout roots and stems, and soon flowers
burst into blossom and dust the air with fine pollen.
At the same time creatures produce their young
and educate them to the ways of the world.

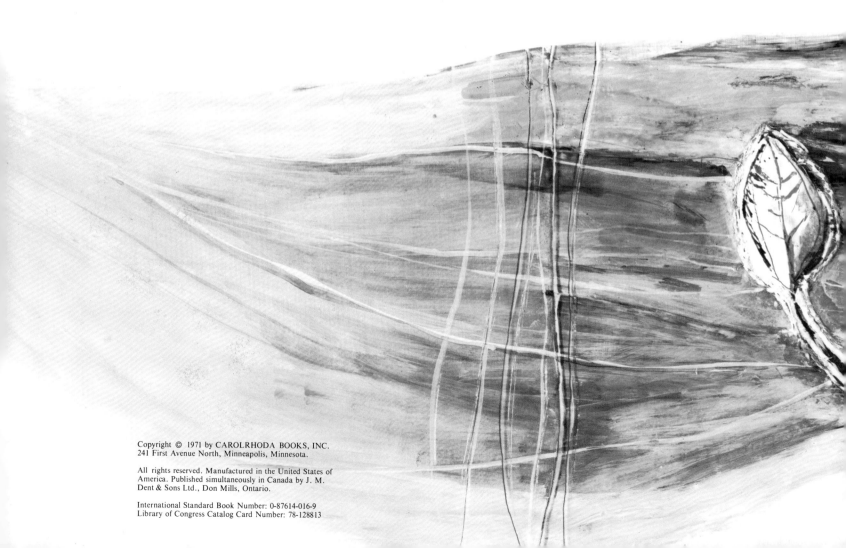

International Standard Book Number: 0-87614-016-9
Library of Congress Catalog Card Number: 78-128813

One spring a young bird was born.
His father taught him how to fly
and then took him to the fields to gather grain.
They flew over the waving grasses from one field
to the next in search of food.

When the little bird became familiar with the countryside,
his father sent him out alone.
"Fly to the fields on the east side of town.
If you do not find food,
fly to the fields on the south side.
When you have found something useful, bring it to me.
Go, and fly with the wind at your back."

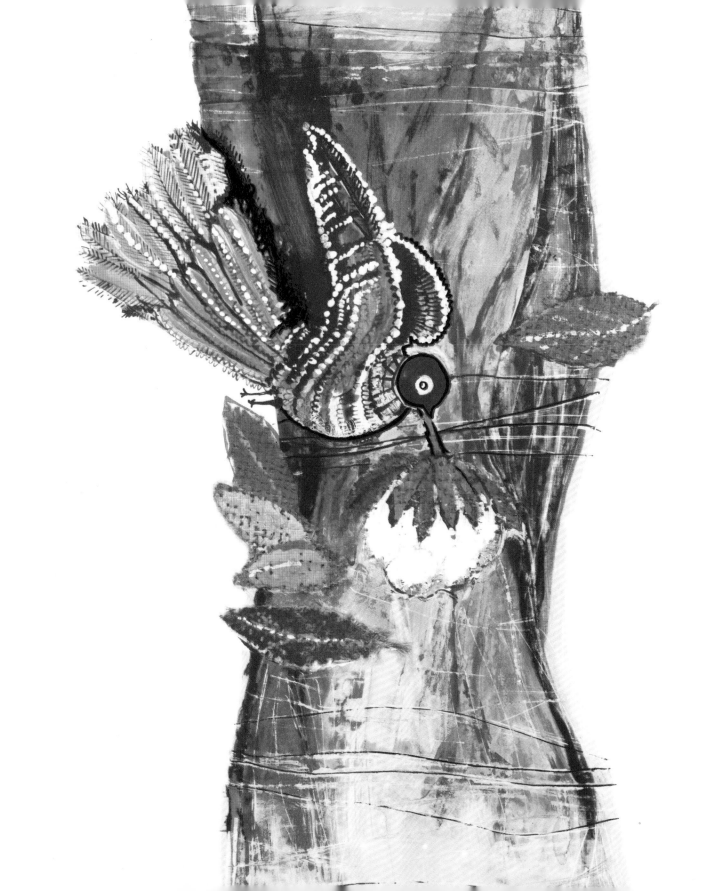

The little bird flew from field to field on the east side
of town but found no food. He flew to the fields
on the south side of town and finally came to one
he had never seen before
He landed to take a closer look. At his feet
he saw a strange plant.
The little bird poked at it with his beak.
It was prickly on the outside and soft on the inside.
But it did not taste like food. This made him curious.
If it wasn't food, what could it be?
He picked it up and flew home.

He showed the soft and prickly plant to his father.
"What do you think it is?" he asked.
"You must find that out for yourself," said his father.
"Go to the spinner's. He will be able to help you."

The little bird flew to the spinner's shop.
When the spinner saw the plant
he said, "Why, you have found a cotton boll.
I will spin its fibers for you."
He took the fluffy white cotton out of its pod
and cleaned it. Then he separated it into strands
that he combed and straightened until they shone.

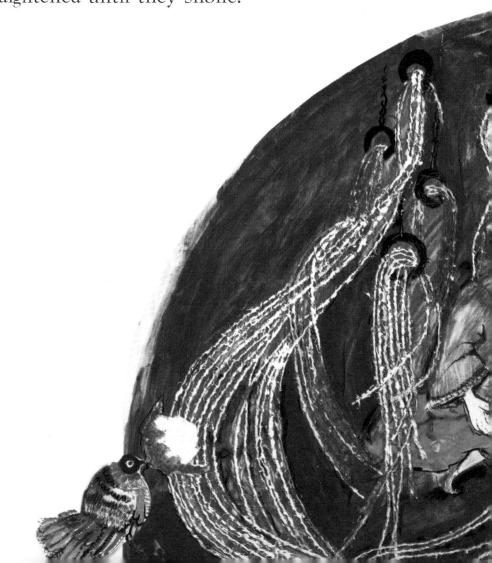

"Now it is ready to spin into yarn," he said.
The spinner picked up a very smooth stick with a
notch at the top. He sat down
and attached the end of a strand in the notch.
Then he rolled the stick against his leg,
turning it faster and faster
until the strands were twisted into yarn.

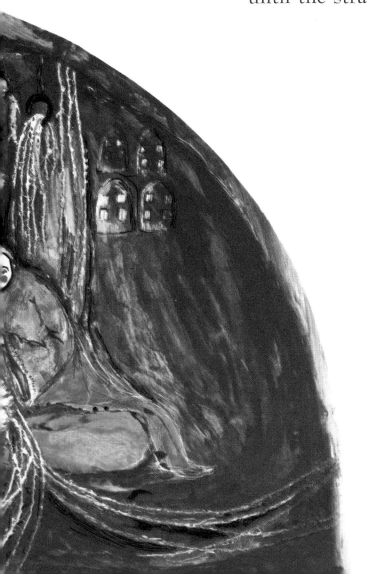

When all the strands had been twisted into yarn,
the spinner said, "What will you give me as payment
for my work?" The little bird thought for a moment.
All he had was the yarn, so he gave half of it
to the spinner and thanked him for his help.
"You must now go to the weaver's shop,"
called the spinner as the little bird flew away.

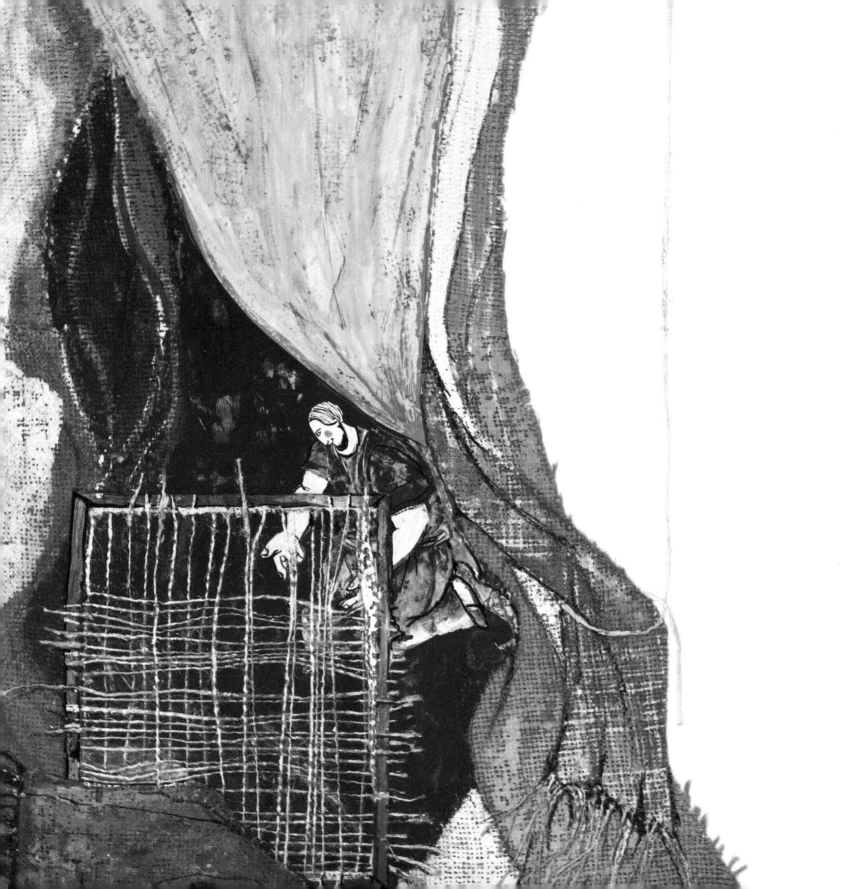

The little bird took his half of the spun yarn
to the weaver. The weaver arranged some of the threads
on the loom, attaching them at the top and the bottom.
Then he laced the rest of the threads
across the loom, over and under the others.
When he finished, the yarn had been woven into cloth.

The weaver said, "What will you pay me
for my weaving?"
"I will give you half of this cloth, "
the little bird said, and he divided the cloth
and gave half to the weaver. He took the
other half and started out the door.
"Now take your cloth to the dyer," said the
weaver, "and he will help you."

In his shop the dyer had seven pots
which he filled with water. Into each pot he put
bark, berries, flowers, leaves, or roots.
They turned the water a bright color. Soon the dyer
had seven different colors of dye in his seven pots.

Then he dipped the little bird's cloth into the first pot.
He waited until it turned the color of the dye
and then dipped it into the next pot.
When he had dipped the cloth in all seven pots,
he hung it up to dry. The colors glowed.

"I have finished," said the dyer
when the cloth was dry.
"How will you pay me
for my trouble?"
The little bird gave him
half of the bright cloth.
"Now go to the dressmaker,"
said the dyer.

When the dressmaker saw the cloth he said,
"What beautiful colors! What wonderful cloth!"
He took it from the little bird and cut off half of it.
"I will take this in payment for my work," he said.
Then he took the bird's piece of cloth and gave it shape
by turning and cutting and sewing.

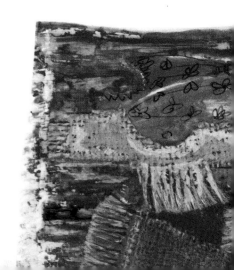

When the dressmaker finished,
the cloth was a brightly colored scarf.
"All this from a soft and prickly cotton boll,"
said the little bird. "I must hurry and show my
father my very grand scarf!"
And off he flew with the wind at his back.